P9-CBT-350

Copyright © 2018 Clavis Publishing Inc., New York

Originally published as *Kwak in het wak* in Belgium and Holland
by Clavis Uitgeverij, Hasselt—Amsterdam, 2017
English translation from the Dutch by Clavis Publishing Inc., New York

Visit us on the Web at www.clavisbooks.com.

No part of this publication may be reproduced or stored in a retrieval system,
or transmitted in any form or by any means, electronic, mechanical, photocopying,
recording, or otherwise, without the prior written permission of the publisher,
except in the case of brief quotations embodied in critical articles and reviews.
For information regarding permissions, write to Clavis Publishing, info-US@clavisbooks.com.

Duck Is Stuck written by Zoubida Mouhssin and illustrated by Pascale Moutte-Bour

ISBN 978-1-60537-415-4

This book was printed in August 2018 at Nikara, M. R. Štefánika 858/25, 963 01 Krupina, Slovenia.

First Edition
10 9 8 7 6 5 4 3 2 1

Clavis Publishing supports the First Amendment and celebrates the right to read.

Zoubida Mouhssin
Pascale Moutte-Baur

DUCK
IS STUCK

Clavis

NEW YORK

Brrr, it's cold up here,
thinks Duck as he flies over the lake.
We still have a long way to travel.
Here is a perfect place to rest.

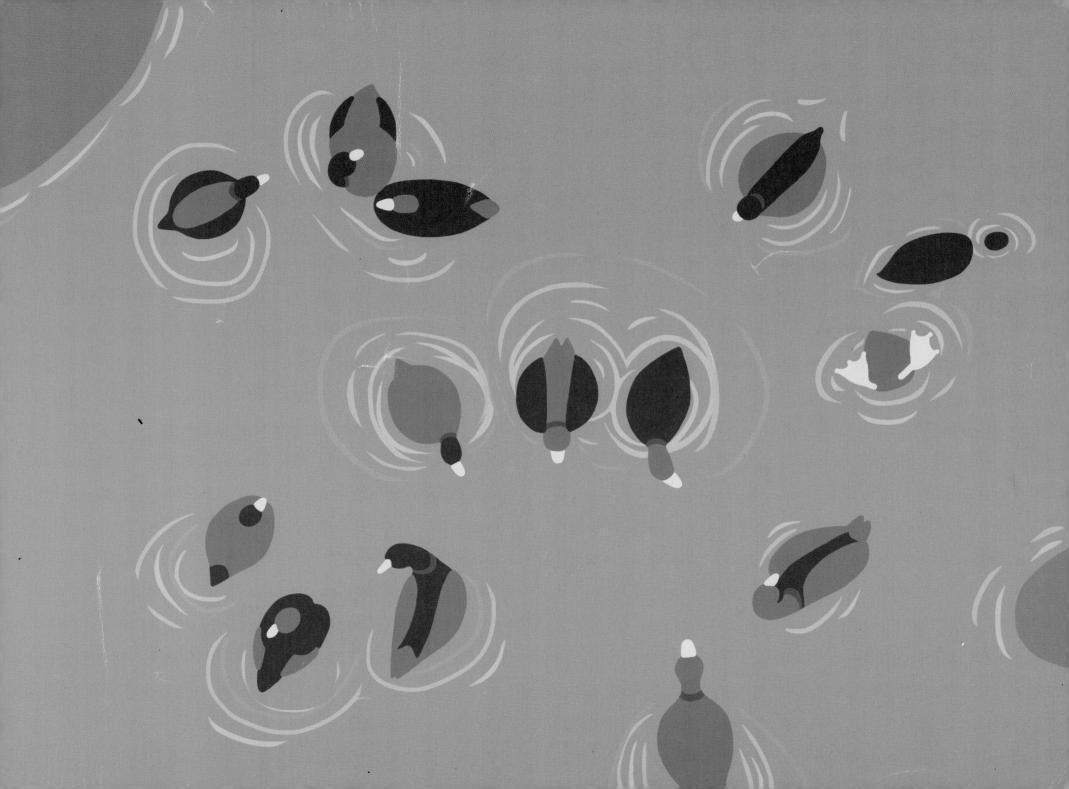

In no time Duck falls asleep.

His sleep is so deep, he doesn't notice it starts snowing . . .

And the lake freezes over.

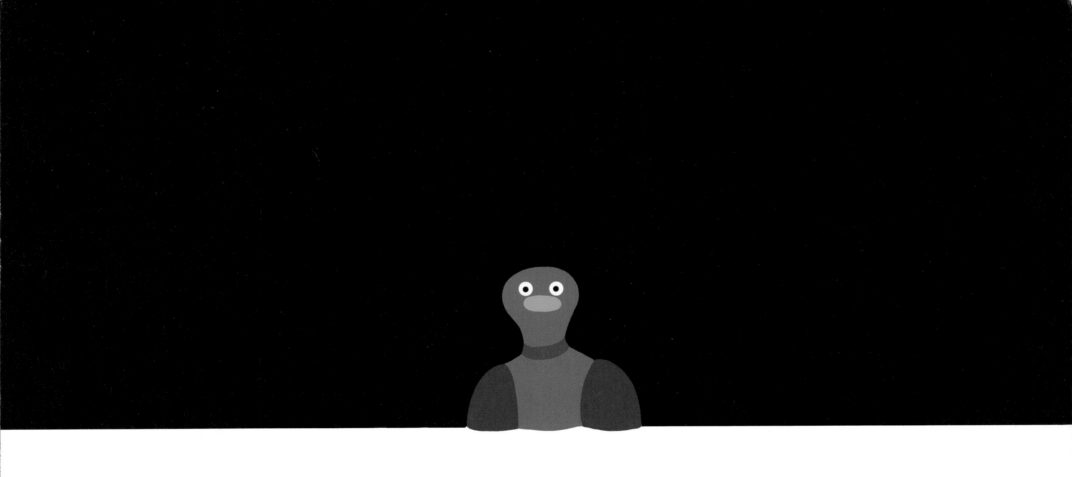

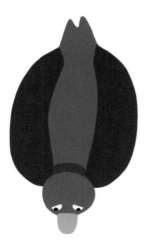

Quack, quack! Duck tries to get free by flapping his wings.
But it's no use. Duck is stuck!

Just then, Duck hears a voice.
"How in the world did you manage to get into that situation?"

It's Snowflake the Rabbit.
"I'm stuck in the ice," Duck explains. "Would you be so kind as to help me?"

Snowflake is happy to try.
  She starts jumping up and down on the ice to make it crack.
    Hop, hop, hop! No luck . . .
      Then Duck hears another voice asking,

"How in the world did you manage to get into that situation?"

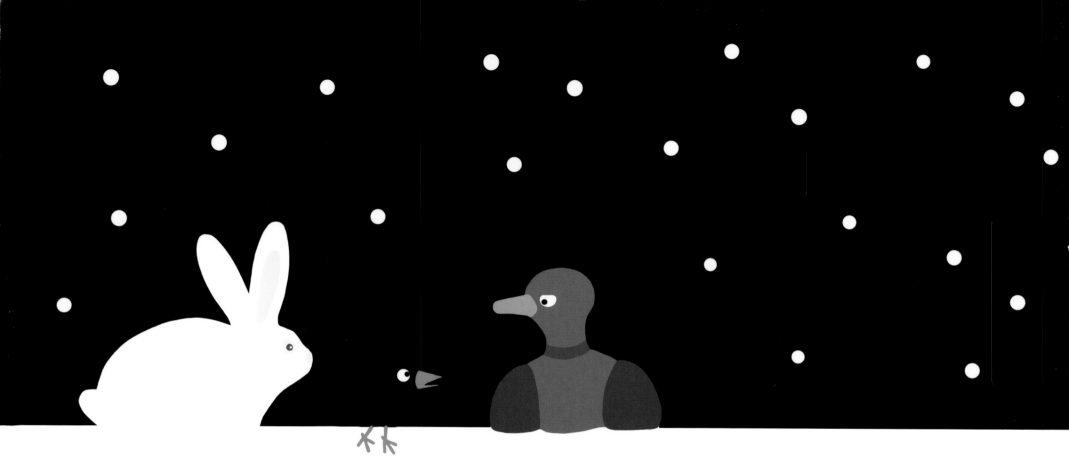

It's Bob the Blackbird.
"Duck is stuck," says Snowflake. "Can you help?"

Bob is happy to try.
He starts pecking his beak into the ice.
Peck, peck, peck! No luck.

Right at that moment there is a loud cracking sound,
followed by a voice asking,
"How in the world did you manage to get into that situation?"

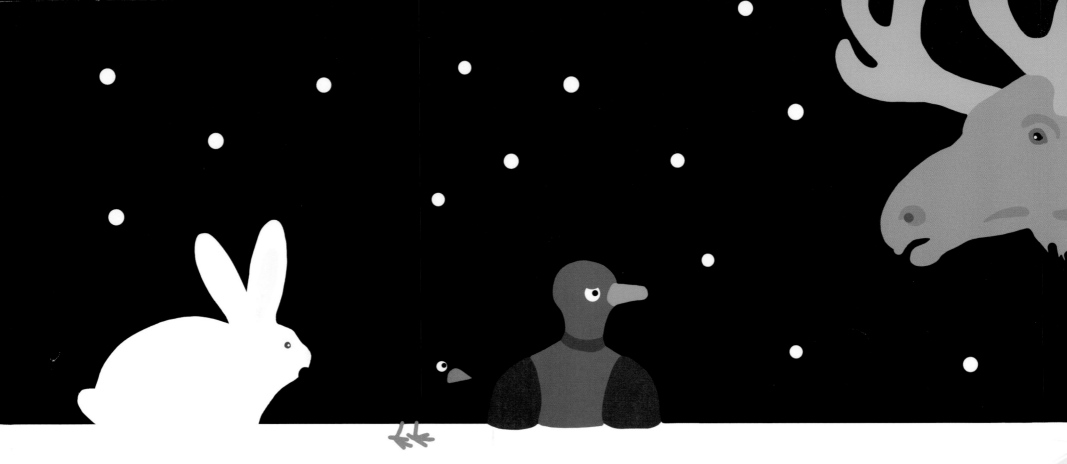

It's Moses the Moose.
"Duck is stuck," say Snowflake and Bob. "Can you help?"
Moose would be happy to try, but he is worried that he will break the ice
and they will all fall in the water.

Duck is worried
that he will be stuck
in the ice forever.

At that very moment he feels something
underneath the ice tickle his webbed feet.

It's Rachel the Rainbow Trout.
"How in the world did you manage to get into that situation?"
Rachel asks.

"Duck is stuck," call Snowflake and Bob and Moses. "Can you help?"
 "I'd be happy to help, but I am too small," says Rachel.

Duck is beginning to think he will never get out of the ice. Then, Rachel has an idea.

She swims to the lodge of Bert the Beaver.

Rachel rings
the doorbell and calls:
"Mister Bert, please come.
Duck is stuck!"

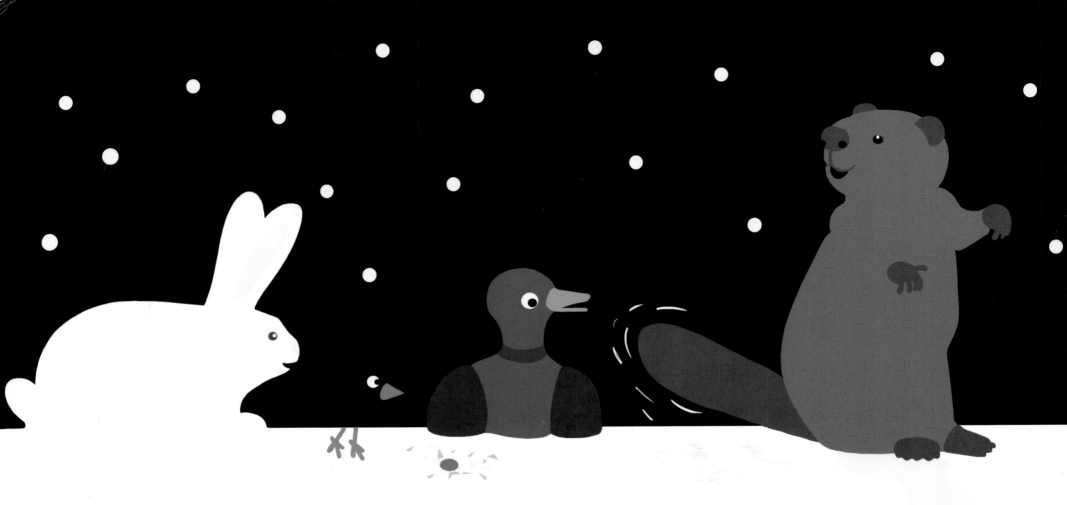

Bert follows Rachel back to Duck. Bert takes one look at Duck and bursts out laughing.
"How in the world did you manage to get into that situation?"

Duck is too tired and cold to even answer.
He just looks down sadly.
"Don't worry, I'm happy to help," Bert says kindly.
And he starts drumming on the ice with his tail.
Bam, bam, bam! No luck.
He tries again. Bam, bam, bam! No luck . . .

Then Snowflake says, "Maybe I can help too?"
"Me too," says Bob. Moses and Rachel want to help as well.

So the beaver, the rabbit, and the blackbird start drumming on the ice together.
The moose and rainbow trout cheer along.
"One, two, three!" **BAM, BAM, BAM!**
Soon there are lots of tiny cracks in the ice.

Duck spreads his wings and . . .
flies right up out of the ice.
Duck is no longer stuck!

Duck flies down
to thank his new friends.

"Well, I still don't understand how you managed to get into that situation," remarks Bert the Beaver. "But, never mind. We are glad we could help." It's late, so Duck flies off and Snowflake, Bob, Moses, and Bert head home.

And Rachel swims back to her children,
who are waiting for a bedtime story.
Perhaps it will be about a duck
who is stuck . . .